THIS WALKER BOOK BELONGS TO:

_____

_____

_____

For Maria and Peter,
Max, Camilla, Anastasia
and Fen

First published 2006 by Walker Books Ltd
87 Vauxhall Walk, London SE11 5HJ

This edition published 2007

2 4 6 8 10 9 7 5 3 1

© 2006 Kim Lewis Ltd

The right of Kim Lewis to be identified as author/illustrator
of this work has been asserted by her in accordance with the
Copyright, Designs and Patents Act 1988

This book has been typeset in Stone Print Roman

Printed in Singapore

British Library Cataloguing in Publication Data: a catalogue
record for this book is available from the British Library

ISBN- 978-1-4063-0503-6

www.walkerbooks.co.uk

A PUPPY for ANNIE

Kim Lewis

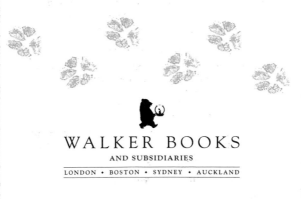

WALKER BOOKS
AND SUBSIDIARIES

LONDON · BOSTON · SYDNEY · AUCKLAND

One day a girl called Annie fell in
love with a puppy called Bess.
"Can I take her home with me?"
asked Annie.

Bess came to a house, only small, on a hill, where the land all around rolled out like the sea. Bess sniffed the air and wagged her tail.

"What is Bess trying to say?" asked Annie.

"Just watch and you'll see," said Mum.

At first, Bess followed Annie wherever she went.

When Annie stopped walking, Bess flopped at her feet.

"What does Bess want?" asked Annie.

"Bess wants to be next to you,"
smiled Mum.

So Annie stroked Bess
and tickled her ears.

Then Bess went snooping around her new house.
She tugged at the pots and pans. She chewed on
the shoes and rolled in the rug.
"What does Bess want?" laughed Annie.
"Bess wants to play with you," said Mum.
So Annie found Bess some toys of her own.

After that, when Mum and Annie
sat down for their lunch, Bess found out
how to say she was hungry. She rattled
her bowl and looked up at Annie.
"I know what you want," said Annie.
So Annie fed Bess and
they ate all together.

Then, when Annie called Bess, she learned to come running. She scratched at the door and sniffed at the boots. She looked up at the hook where Annie's coat hung. Annie knew what Bess wanted most of all in the world. "Time to go out," she said to her dog.

Bess leapt a lot, full of nothing but joy.
So did her best friend Annie.
They ran every day to their wild
special places, where a girl and her
dog knew just where to go.
And the world, right then,
belonged to Bess and Annie.

But one day as they sat down
to rest, Annie told Bess she
would be going to school soon.
Annie stroked Bess for as long
as she could. Mum was glad
to see them when they
came home again.

Then the day came and
Annie was gone.
Bess tried hard to say
what she wanted.
She trotted after Mum while
Mum did her work.
She played with her toys and
ate all her lunch.
She scratched at the door.
She sniffed at the boots.
She stared at the hook where
Annie's coat wasn't.

Bess ran to Mum and lay at her feet.
"Annie won't be long," said Mum.
She gently stroked Bess and tickled her ears.
Bess curled in a ball.
She waited in sleep.
She didn't know any
more how to say what
she wanted.

Then, at the sound of the old
school bus, Bess leapt a lot,
full of nothing but joy.
She ran to Annie without
being called. She wagged
her tail hard. She wagged
all over. Mum gave Annie
a great big hug.
"What does Bess want?"
laughed Mum.
"Bess wants me!" Annie
said to her dog.

So Bess and Annie went walking together. And the world, right then, all over again, belonged to just Bess and Annie.

WALKER BOOKS BY KIM LEWIS

FLOSS • JUST LIKE FLOSS

EMMA'S LAMB • SHEPHERD BOY • FRIENDS

THE LAST TRAIN • LITTLE BAA

MY FRIEND HARRY • GOODNIGHT HARRY

HERE WE GO, HARRY • HOORAY FOR HARRY